Giulio Zoni

A Visit to Belgirate Lago Maggiore

J. Canessa's Hotel Borromeo - Excursion-guide on the Lake Verbano

Giulio Zoni

A Visit to Belgirate Lago Maggiore
J. Canessa's Hotel Borromeo - Excursion-guide on the Lake Verbano

ISBN/EAN: 9783337382636

Printed in Europe, USA, Canada, Australia, Japan

Cover: Foto ©Andreas Hilbeck / pixelio.de

More available books at **www.hansebooks.com**

A VISIT

TO

BELGIRATE

LAGO MAGGIORE

(J. CANESSA'S HOTEL BORROMEO)

EXCURSION - GUIDE

ON THE LAKE VERBANO

BY

JULIUS CAESAR ZONI

MILAN

GUGLIELMINI 'S TYPOGRAPHY

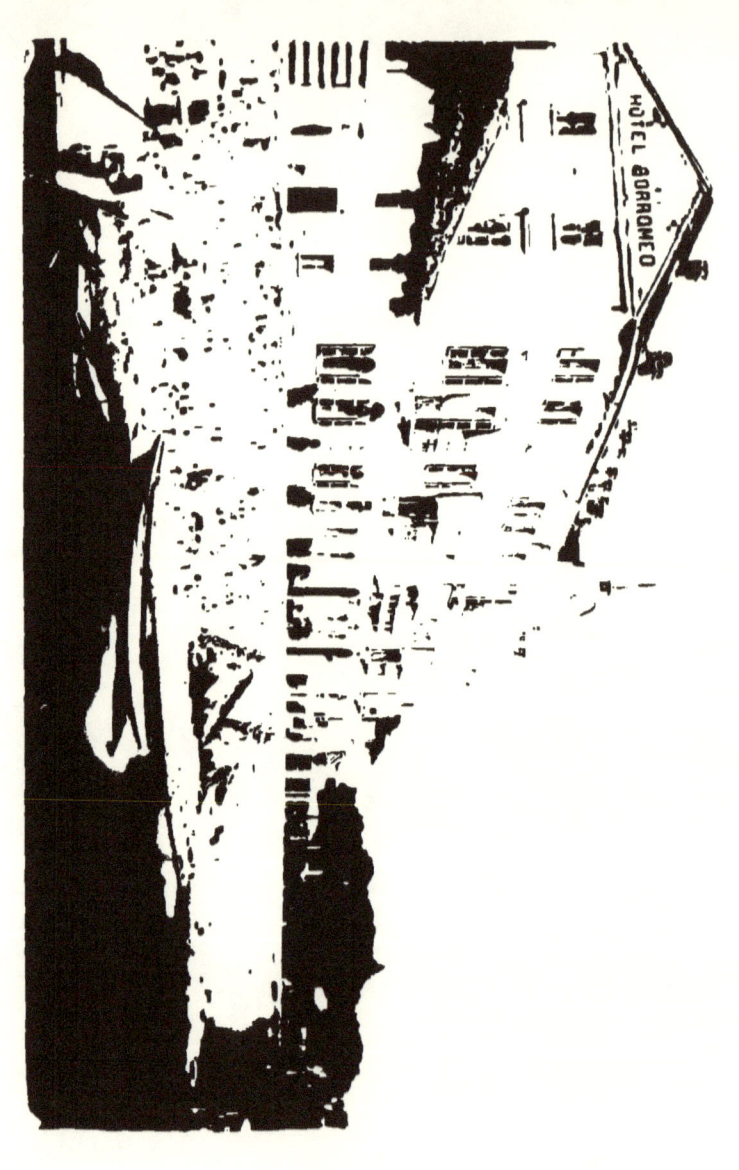

A VISIT TO BELGIRATE

No matter from what point of the world
you come, when you arrive at Arona, a small
and very ancient town, the origin of which
is lost in the whirlpools of time, you are
touched and agreably surprised in looking
around you. On one side you see the gran-
deur of an immense gulf of the blue Verbano; on the other, your eye may discern small
hills and high mountains with ondulated summits. On your right, boroughs and villages
and ruins of embattled castles, hundreds
and hundreds of beautiful buildings and monuments; on your left, houses and palaces,

and then Borromeo's castle on St. Charles Mountain, and the remains of the primitive castle where the Saint was born, his temple and his colossal statue, which rises high over the mountain. If you enter that statue and step up to its head, you will enjoy a charming and extended view.

After seing, at a glance, buildings, hotels, theatre and the church of St. Mary (of XV century), which is also interesting because of G. Ferrari and Appiani's appreciated paintings, you can embark upon the steam-boat which you will find waiting at the dock, and plies to and fro regularly from one end of the lake to the other, from south to north *.

* Thirty five streams, at least, without calculating brooks and rivulets, are the affluents of that lake, the surface of which is about 216,000,000 square meters, when it is 2 meters above the hydrometer of Pallanza; its length, from Magadino to Sesto-Calende, is 66,000 m., the maximum of its latitude is 12,000 m. from Laveno to Feriolo, and the medium of it is calculated to be from one to five kilom.; however, bewteen Arona and Angera, it is but one kilom. — The elevation of the lake, compared with that of the Adriatic is valued 794 m. to zero at the hydrometer of Pal-

Now, from the poop of the boat, take a last glance at the town you leave behind you, and the *Aronensia castra* will appear to you like a majestuous amphitheatre which, from the coast, seems to salute you and, smiling, say — We shall see again. —

lanza, and its gratest depth (between Luino and Intra) is 934 m. That of the Lake of Como is but 604. — The Lake Maggiore is situated between $23.^0 9.'$ and $26.^0 31.'$ East-long., from the meridian of Iron-Island; or betwcen $6.^0 9.'$ and $6.^0 31.'$ from the meridian of Paris; and betwen $45.^0 43.$ and $46.^0 10.'$ north.-lat. —

It is not unworth mentionning that, on 3.d October 1868, the water rose till 7. 60 meters above the hydrometer of Pallanza, so that, every where on the coast, incalculable losses were suffered from the sudden innundation, which, very luckily lasted for a short time.

The water of the lake is clear and pure, sky-colored and very eificatious for haths. It abounds in fish like *agoni*, trouts, eels and others of less importance. Should the tourist wish to have a general view of the lake, he must ascend to the top of the Gallona, a mountain which rises close to Treffiume; and this is a Village on the way to the *Orrido di Sant'Anna*. (See **Cannobio**, p. 11). —

In a while you are at Angera, Meina, Lesa, Belgirate which will soon receive our visit; then comes Stresa and *Isola Bella* (Beautiful-Island), the perfumed queen of the whole lake; a little farther, you will find Baveno and Feriolo, which almost surronuds the *Isola Superiore* or Isola de' Pescatori (Superior-Isle or the Fishers-Isle); the boat then turns to Suna, then to Pallanza the beloved little town of the *Isolino di San Giovanni* (St. John's little Isle) which rises to adorn with its charms the beauty of that ancient place; its hotel actually appears to you like the Palace of enchantments.

If you could stop there for a while, you would see, from one side

D'un mare interminabile il cospetto

(The aspect of the boundless sea)

from the other', a new Eden. But you must continue your way to Intra, *the small Manchester of the lake*, and afterwards, cross to the opposite Laveno, which lies at the feet of the mountain called the *Sasso di ferro* (Iron stone) about 1084 meters high, from the summit of which you may enjoy such an agreable view, that it

« Leva di terra al ciel nostro intelletto »

(raises our mind from earth to heaven)

Now, let us go on to Porto-Valtravaglia which we'll meet at our right-hand, then to the opposite Ghiffa which seems to project in the waters with an intention to point out, the middle of the lake or to give you a hand, while you are passing, and tell you

Come il raggio del sole ognor mi bacia,
Si leggiadra e gentil quale mi vedi
Non m'obbliare, o passeggier cortese,
Un saluto ed un bacio a me tu porta.

(The sun-beams come and give me their daily kiss and J am always, such as thou seest me, charming and graceful; do not forget me, then, courteous traveller, when thou passest, and give me a salute and a kiss.)

Now, here is Oggebbio, a little place adorned with beautiful palaces and agreable villas, the

best of which is prof. G. Polli's *Solitudine* (soli-
tude); here is also the mild *Nizza of the lake*
i. e. Cannero, a very wholesome place even
in winter *; if you turn then to the East, you
will see the celebrated and busy Luino the
native country of Bernardino Luini called the
Raffaello of the Lombard School (1460-1550).
In coming back, if you remain there for some
days, you will hear the exploits of Garibaldi
and see his marble statue whereon you would
like to read: To *the hero of the two worlds;
the Luinese***. A few minuts after, you will pass
by *Macagno Inferiore* and *Superiore,* two twin
villages parted by the waters of the Giona;
the former of them, by the remains of its
ancient castle, calls to your mind the splen-
dour and arrogance of the ancestors, and

* When the traveller visits Cannero, he must
not forget inquiring about the famous tale of the
banditti Mazzardi or Mazzarditi; he should like-
wise visit the castle *La Malpaga.*

** This statue, a work of the distinguished sculp-
tor Putinati, was erected in 1867. It represents
the dreaded General layng hold of his sword; it
is 3 meters high, and placed upon a pedestal
about four meters high. —

tells you rather boastingly that the German Otho the great was living there in 932.
The boat cutting the foaming water brings you to Cannobio, where you may have one of the best views of the lake; you may see also *the Orrido di Sant'Anna* and the well known hydrotherapic establishment *La Salute* (The health), erected by Dr. Fossati-Barbò (1867-69) and, moreover, the bramantic pictures and the frescoes of the above mentioned Ferrari. Soon after, you pass over the line, which, though unperceived, indicates the political limits of Italy and Switzerland; this line goes from Val-Mara, at the West, to Pino and Cavajano, at the East. Here you may visit Brissago (Riva Ticinese - in the Tessin Canton) which affords many and interesting pecularities; leaving then behind you the little *Isles of S. Pancrazio o dei Conigli* (of rabbits) opposite to Ronco, you see Ascona a small town of longobard origin.

Now if, crossing the mouth of the river Maggia, you take a turn around the large promontory of Ascona, the scene suddenly changes and becomes more agreable; in fact, here is a rich and nice little town, called Locarno, the capital of the Tessin-Canton. The populous and ancient Locarno (probably from *Loc-ar-no* place on the waters. 12000 inhab.), the native country of many celebrated men, certainly contains many things both ancient and worth being seen, but we cannot stay because the boat must hurry to its last station Magadino.

This is an unwholesome and unlucky district, but it has the advantage of being the deposit of the goods which are imported from Switzerland to Italy and viceversa.

During these six hours, you had the pleasure of admiring the magnificent and varied scenes of the lake. Now you leave the large mouth of the Tessin, and while you are returning, give a special attention to the places, which you think particularly worth being seen and remembered, and, as you arrive at Belgirate, descend and stay, for it is the principal object of our *visit*.

Belgirate! Whether you look at this charming seat from the lake or from the opposite shore, on the steep rock of which lies the smiling Ispra, or from the top of *the Sasso Ballaro*, which you will find a little farther, or from the hermitage of S. Catherine, it always appears to you gracefully seated among green trees and delightful gardens, caressed, from the break of day to evening, by a mild and gentle breeze: oh! Belgirate

È il variopinto mazzolin di fiori,
Che l'onde e l'aura qui profuma ognor.

(is the many coloured nosegay that perfumes the wave and the breeze).

The delicious appearance of this chief place (Belgirate or *girate-bello* = take a nice turn) is still increased by its positions; it was built upon a small promontory between the two gay villages of Sesa and Stresa, which are at a short but unequal distance from it; the former being only ten minuts distant and the latter nearly half an hour; should you wish to take a walk to those villages, the wide and agreable road of the Simplon will lead you there and, on your way, you will have, from one side, the blue lake, and from the other, villas, gardens and parks.

The mildness of the climate, the salubrity of the air, the peculiar gracefulness of the

surrounding hills, made of Belgirate a celebrated sojourn, so that distinguished doctors
declared that it is one of the best places
where strangers may yo every year to divert
themselves and get healthy *.

When you come from the port, which is
constructed upon a platform leading to the
high way, you almost face a magnificent building whereon you can read: **Hotel Borromeo** **. The landlord, Mr. John Canessa,

* It is statet that all those who, being unheal-
thy, came to Belgirate, had their health perfectly
restored when they came away some months after.
So that they never forgot the agreablenees of that
healthy coutry-side, nor the remarkable kindness
of the poeple, and above all, the solicitude with
which M.r John Canessa took care of them as
long as they were in his Hotel. — The annual
visits that some of those persons pay him, and
letters of thanks coming from every direction are
the best proof of the fact.

** Before 1870, there was, in this place a lonely
and little inn. with stables and sheepfold, a shed
and a coach-house; it was a post-stand for the
change of horses, when the counts Borromeo went
to their Isles on the lake Maggiore or to other
feudal territories, and it remained so as long as

presents himself to you and, receiving you in
the most engaging manner, he politely decla-
res to be at your service. As soon as you

the inhabitants of those country-sides could not
avail themselves of rail-road-conveniences. The
actual palace, which is called **Hotel Borromeo**, had been better called **Hotel Canessa**
or **Belgirate**, inorder to avoid confounding it
with the *Hotel of Borromeo-Isles* at Stresa, as it
was often the case. Canessa's Hotel Borromeo *at
Belgirate* has many halls on the ground-floor,
and not less than 95 rooms, and elegant closets,
which open either towards the lake or upon the
gardens. Every appartment is adorned with very
convenient and rich furnitures; the best comfort,
ease and quiet are here to be found by strangers
and families.

Every thing is disposed in such way as to sa-
tisfy anybody's taste, and you can find out any
pastime whatever. There is good biliards, a con-
fortable and well provided reading room, newspapers of different countries, hand-books, travel-
and history-books, written in foreign languages;
also pianoes and music of any kind whatever,
and, moreover, neat cabinets for cold or hot-baths
in the wholesome water of the lake. The Hotel
is open to the strangers' convenience all the year.

arc comfortably seated, you proceed to sa-
tisfy the good appetite, which the pure air
of the place has given you; then you take a
room on the first floor, but as all the appartments opening towards the lake arc already
occupied, you are obliged to take a room
opening into the gardens. You may however
visit all the appartments at some hours of the
day. From the top of this building, you can

Bedecked small boats and pretty canoos are always at the service of those who would like to
visit the peculiarities of the neighbouring coasts.
Rich carriages and many horses are always ready
for excursions; you may go, if you like until the
Simplon or the lake of Orta. You can find also
Guides for the Motterone. The service is unbla-
mable and the prices are regularly fixed. Here
you find, in short, such conveniences as you cannot find in every other establishment of that kind.
And these conveniences attract many families,
that are much satisfied even with the victuals,
and they agree, therefore. with the proprietor on
taking their board in his Hotel during the whole
year or month by month, week by week. The
price is about 8 frs. according the appartment
and the position of the rooms.

enjoy a still better panorama than that you admired when you left Arona. On the first floor, entering the central hall, you go out on a large balcony whence your eye can expatiate on the road of the Simplon and on the nicest basin of the lake, which looks like a limpid mirror, and in which are reflected all the surrounding lands, from Sesto-Calende to Pallanza and Intra and nearly until Ghiffa at your right hand. If you look down from the balcony, your eye will be delighted at the sight of an agreable and comfortable terrace-garden, placed beyond the road and near the lake; for the skilful landlord has done all in his power to adorn his hotel in the most agreable way in order it should present the best conveniences to the strangers. Every thing in this garden is set in good order and with a good taste. Beds of flowers adorned with large flower-pots and with many and different plants, which invite you to take place under their shady branches. And, indeed, the place looks very much like a saloon in the open air, under the smiling shy; there you may sit down in good society either to dine or play, which is particularly agreable among

*

the peculiar beauties which Natnre has be-
stowed to that beautiful and privileged region
of Italy.

This terrace is enclosed in a railing and a
marblé-parapet. Hence, by a flight of marble-
stairs, you can reach the shore whether you
have a mind to go on boat or to shut yourself in a small wooden lodge and give yourself the pleausure of a bath, or jump into the
water and exercise yourself in swimming. If,
by chance, you cast a look at the hotel from
the boat, you will remark with complacency
its oriental side, adorned with its ninety win-
dows; the proprietor, however, is going to
enlarge his hotel; for the concourse of stran-
gers |and visiters is growing every year in
that wholesome country.

Now, come back to the hotel, and observe
the chambers, closets and halls, and note how
perfectly the wooden floors and the mosaic
works are made. The halls on the ground-
floor, opening towards the lake, may be, at
need, converted into one large saloon for ex-
traordinary meetings or dinners. Besides the
rich furnitures, there is something else deser-
ving your attention: no common pictures nor

vain and useless figures are exposed to your
sight; but thirty five works of value which
call to your mind the well-known name of
the modern *GuidoReni*, the lamented Andrea
Appiani (1761-1817) whom the prince of poets,
Parini (1729-1799), celebrated in his verses.
Those thirty five works are the appreciated
engravings of Longhi, Benaglia, Bisi and Rosaspina; they exactly reproduce Napoleon's
exploits, which were so finely and artfully
painted by Appiani. Mr Canessa's purpose in
adorning so carefully his halls is to afford
the visiters an opportunity for useful conver-
sation on the most important subjects of modern history, and to demonstrate, by those
scenes, the truth of Mme d'Epinay's remarkable maxim: *Dans les tableaux de l'histoire,
on voit combattre et tomber des géants, puis
naître et se jouer des pygmées.*
In the reading-room, after reviewing the
newspapers and all the volumes which you
will find carefully ranged upon the tables or
in their shelves, you will no doubt think that
this will be of great use to you after a long
walk or pastime; here you will find both instruction and relief, even if you were obliged to

read a book for the second time, for Voltaire's maxim is true: *En lisant, pour la première fois, un bon livre, on doit éprouver le même plaisir que si on faisait un nouvel ami; relire un livre qu'on a lu, c'est un ancien ami qu'on revoit.*

Come away now, and leave gentlemen and ladies to their own occupations; as soon as you are out, cross the yards and come to the pensile garden of the hotel. The yard leading to it, is overshaded by american vines, so that even in the heat of the day, you can enjoy the most agreable fresh-air and pass delicious hours with a numerous and gay society.

By two flights of steps you get to the garden; this is indeed a true *jardin-potager*, laid out upon a small hill and surrounded with an enclosure. Alleys, beds of flowers and fruits, plots of greens and kitchen fruits, all that makes of this garden a pleasant rendez-vous. Apart, on the same hill, you will find an artificial little mountain adorned with different plants; here too you are pleased at the freshness of the air, which allows you to sit down for a reading or to take nice walks through romantic and winding alleys. When, from this eminence, you look at the lake and the surrounding green hills, and then at the picturesque landscape around you, you cannot help being moved, and you should like to continue ascending. Therefore, an issue from the enclosure is open to you, and they lead you, by a narrow and steep road called *the Calvary*, to the old church of *Santa Maria Vecchia;* behind the church is the cemetery of Belgirate. From this eminence, what a magical view! You would stay there for ever. At a short distance below, you meet with the nice village of Belgirate, which displays before your eyes its charming beauties; pretty small houses, gardens and parks adorn the graceful slope of the hill until the road; here, the palaces gardens and houses form a line along the road until beyond Hotel Borromeo. Every thing looks so nice and elegant that you feel attracted to visit many and many of those seats. As to public establishments nothing is wanting; work-houses, shops of all kinds, pharmacies, restaurants, coffee-houses; public schools, asylums etc. For the latter, the Belgiratese are much beholden to the generosity and maternal affection of the distinguished lady Helen Conelli *. The post-road, protected by a parapet on the lake-side, is the principal walk and the best rendez-vous for the poeple of the place and for those who are enjoying the pleasures of the country. If you follow the road until he Hotel, you will pass before the parish-church, the steeple of which is reflected by the lake; the appreciated organ of this church is also a gift of M.ʳ Conelli's. Now, instead of stopping at the Hotel, let us continue our walk and stop, shortly after, before the first country-seat which particularly attracts the attention of

* On the left of the *Chiesa Vecchia* (Old Church) and near the entrance of the church-yard, are two Monuments; one of them was erected to the most distinguished family Cavallini, and the other to the famili Conelli. — Helen Conelli died 1863.

The Belgiratese will ever keep a good remembrance of the defunct Joseph Conelli, who did so much good to their country, not neglecting anything to provide the children with a good education inorder they ishould prove men of value, according the maxim of Helvetius — *Nothing is impossible to education.*

travellers; here, the lombard and modern Cornelia and her sons, the Gracchi of the restored Italy, came, from time to time, and spent their leisure-hours; here, in 1869, John Cairoli, mortally wounded by the enemy's arms, bid a last farewell to his beloved country! To perpetuate this mournful event, the following words of the ardent philosopher and writer, F. D. Guerrazzi *, were engraved on a stone placed on the entrance:

QUANDO LA SOLITUDINE DI QUESTA CASA TI PERCUOTA LA MENTE

O BENEDETTO CAIROLI

PENSA

DATO A POCHISSIMI SUPERARE LA MORTE

LA MADRE TUA E I FRATELLI IMMORTALI

PERCHÈ IMMORTALE LA RELIGIONE DI COLORO

[CHE SACRARONSI INTERI

ALLA PATRIA E ALL'UMANITA'

E CONSÓLATI.

I BELGIRATESI DECRETARONO QUESTA MEMORIA IN ONORANZA DELLA CORNELIA E DEI FABÎ LOMBARDI ANNO 1872, 1.º AGOSTO.

---

* Francis Dominic Guerrazzi one of the first who began to write historic novels in Italy, was

But let us drive away melancholy and resume our walk; here is now the beautiful villa of countess Mestiatis-Castellengo; then the most elegant villa of countess Biscaretti, and the capricious *Chalet* of minister Bonghi. Somewhat farther on, you will no doubt stop before another charming villa and visit it, for it is a new paradise. It is called **Villa Danovaro.** Some years ago it belonged to the illustrious marquis of Brême and was called *Villa dei due riali* on account of two little torrents, which pass through it from its upper end down to the lake. The actual proprietor, M.ʳ Danovaro from Genoa, made, with it, something like a garden of the Hesperides, a new sojourn of Calypso, but far more beautiful. Wherever you may direct your steps,

a most eminent man of letters, the giant of the giants of liberty; he was born in 1805 at Leghorn and died in 1873 on 23 September at his *Villa Cinquantina nel Fitto di Cecina*, close to Leghorn. *The Siege of Florence*, a creation which is universally known, was written in the prisons of the State, in the fortress *Stella di Portoferrajo* where Guerrazzi had been confined, charged with the crime of loving his country (1834).

you find numerous traces of the fertility of the soil and, at the same time, you observe that it is cultivated with care and that every thing is kept with great diligence. Here, indigenous and exotic plants, shrubs of different kinds and zones, are growing vigorously and abundantly, and adorn beautiful grass-plots and beds of flowers. If, on one side, you admire Flora's rich vestry, you are struck at seing, on the other, such beautiful and high trees as pines, firs, laurels of all kinds, and the like. Every now and then, you stop before a plant of a different sort; and you will perhaps remark with wonder that the plants coming from the torrid zone are so perfectly acclimated that they do not suffer at all, in the cold season. The reason of it is clear enough: the Alps prevent the north-wind from blowing over this country. — After so overrunning and going about on every side; after passing through many labyrints and over many nice little valleys, brooks and foaming turrents; after seing some fine grots in the most recòndite corners of the property, and different basins from which spout graceful *jets-d'eau*, you arrive at a large esplanade, one half of which is almost entirely occupied by a long and quadrangular fish-pond in which cheerfully glide silvery and gold-coloured small fishes; from a rocky spot in the middle of it, spouts another magnificent *jet-d'eau*, which rises very high and falls again like drizzling rain. Around this reservoir are placed fine marble-statues representing the four poetic deities: *Spring*, *Summer*, *Autumn*, and *Winter*; and besides: *Europe*, *Asia*, *Africa* and *America*. The rest of the esplanade has been adapted for gymnastic and other pastimes of that kind. Here too you are delighted with a cooling zephyr that mixes itself up with the sweet odor of flowers and with the fragrance of herbs and trees. — But let us continue our way, for we must now visit nice little *chalets* and fictitious ruins of ancient castles, cottages or other curious buildings; take care, however; for, while your mind and eyes are entirely fixed on those things; while you get on amidst some shady bushes and follow one of those numerous and solitary alleys; while you stop and gaze delightfully at a rich vine-arbour or other peculiarities of the place, it may happen that you find yourself suddenly sprinkled from every side by some invisible water-spouts, which, springing from earth, fall again upon you, so that you come out fairly wet. When you have so paid that familiar, but not always agreable tribute, we resume our walk upon a flowered grass which breathes out a very sweet odor and looks as if it would tell you in its tender language. — Don't tread upon these flowers, if you take so much delight in them:

Non calpestarci, se ti siam cortesi;

and, indeed, at every step, you are obliged, not without sorrow, to walk upon some of those lively beings; for, as Bernardin de Saint-Pierre said, we pay more attention to a flower than to a star, and take much more interest in a little garden, than in the whole firmament. And at the sight of these lovely beings,

Di soäve ristoro a quei che passa,

you are tenderly affected with pleasure and feel as if you could'nt come away from that

charming sojourn. At all events, you know
that you will never forget

    *Le elette cose che il bel loco serra. *   **c**

(the selected things that the beatificul place contains).

We come out, then, with regret and, if you
like, we'll walk on towards Stresa and visit
other large and small villas, which are the
most admired things of this coast of the lake.
First, comes a beautiful building, which is
yet in construction and will be the pleasant
summer-house of the rich family Palestrini.
Its architecture, as far as we can judge at
present, gives us a favorable idea of M.^{r} De- **4**
fendente Vanini's architectural talent. Then
comes the extended Villa Fulvia, which for-
merly belonged to the princess Matilda Bonaparte; then the pretty Vignolo belonging to
an english gentleman, Mr Nixon, and, within a
few steps, the graceful Villa Pallavicini en-
closing delightful beauties. Let us go on, however; our walk is not yet over. Following the
rout, we arrive at Stresa, a delicious sojourn
too, both for the natives and those who en-

joy themselves in the country; its buildings are admirable. The large and elegant hotel too; it is situated beyond the magnificent Villa and park of H. R. H. the duchess of Genoa, the mother of the beloved and reverenced **Princess Margaret**, who will soon be the most precious gem of the crown of Italy.

Now, while you are coming back, observe how many places you have yet to visit, and you will perceive that your *visit to Belgirate* is not finished, and that you will have every day some nice turn to take or other curious things to see. And don't mind the time and fatigue you are spending in such walks, for *voyager, c'est apprendre.*

Travellers, and especially, tourist wrote that Belgirate is the centre of agreable walks, the rendez-vous of Nature and Art, where we can admire that luxuriant display of divine harmony, which will ever be the greatest delight of a noble mind, of a mind which, even in its pastimes, scarches the beautiful and the instruction. Then, if you stop at Belgirate, don't fail going out at early dawn, and hasten up to the top of a high mountain, and you will enjoy a magnificent spectacle. You will contemplate, on one side, the elevated and ondulated snowy summits of the Alps, which confine the horizon, and, on the other, a boundless rosy-sky, which smiles to you so cordially that you wish you had a pair of wings inorder you might fly far away and see all it covers. But go out in the afternoon too, or in the evening, and visit, once more, and more carefully all you have already seen in a hurry. You will perceive that though Belgirate may not afford to its visiters neither historical remembrances of remote ancestors, nor relics of ancient churches, nor museums, nor any trace of heathen temples; it unfolds however, before you, and with a noble pride, its activity, its industry and commerce, the fertility of its soil, from which the skilful and intelligent country-men draw the most excellent fruits and wine.

In short, Belgirate is a small but very important chief-place, which rapidly acquired its actual renown by rivaling with the neighbouring lands with a noble emulation. And they all, disdaining indolence, agreed among themselves and engraved on their arms the three ❶ of Theodore de Bèze to symbolize their common principles — **Opus, Opes, Ops** — i. e. Labor, Wealth and Care, which is explained well enough in Franklin's maxim: — Don't sleep to much or you'll become poor; rise early and you will have fortune and health.

O Italian people, imitate your countrymen!

THE END

EIN BLICK NACH BELGIRATE

LAGO MAGGIORE

BELGIRATE

LAGO MAGGIORE (ITALIEN)

(GROSSER SEE)

GASTHOF BORROMEO VON JOHANN CANESSA

———

REISEBEGLEITER
AUF DEM VERBANO

von

JULIUS CÄSAR ZONI

—◄●►—

MAILAND
BUCHDRUCK GUGLIELMINI

EIN BLICK NACH BELGIRATE

An den malerischen Ufern des romantischen
Verbano liegt die kleine alterthümliche Stadt
Arona, deren Ursprung sich im Wirbel der
Zeit verliehrt; welch bezaubernder Anblick;
hier der grenzenlose Meerbusen des himmel-
blauen Verbano; dort Hügeln und hohe Berge,
welche ihre Spitzen in den Wolken verlieh-
ren; rechts Marktflecken und Dörfer, Ueber-
bleibe von alterthümlichen Schlössern, Denk-
mälern und Gräbern; links Lustschlösser und
Häuser und das Lehngut Borromeo auf dem
Berge San Carlo (heiliger Karl) die Ruinen
dieses ehemaligen Schloses ist der Geburtsort

des Heiligen (Karl Borromeo, Erzbischof von Mailand 1538 — 1584) noch seine riesenmässige Bildsäule, hoch 1084 m.

Ein wirklich bezauberndes Panorama bietet sich dem Auge im Gipfel der Säule dar, von wo man die günstigste Aussicht auf den See in seiner ganzen Länge und seine herrlichen Umgebungen geniesst, weshalb auch dieser Punkt von allen Besuchern benützt wird. Nachdem man so Schlösser, Theater und die Pfarrkirche Santa Maria (15 Iahrhundert) mit ihren berühmten Gemälde von G. Ferrari und Appiani bewundert hat, nimmt man ein Schiff um die See von einem Strande zum andern, südlich bis nördlich, durchlaufen zu können *. — Vom Schiffe aus noch einen

* Wenigstens 35 Flüsse ohne die kleineren zu zählen, ergiessen in diesen See, seine Oberfäche ist ungefähr 216,000,000 m. q. wenn er sich 2 m. über die Wasserwage von Pallanza befindet, seine Länge von Magadino bis Sesto-Calende zählt 66,000, die grösste Breite 12,000 von Laveno bis Feriolo, mittelmässige 4—5 kilometer. Von Arona bis Angera ist nur 1 kilom. Entfernung. Die Erhebung des Verbano verglichen mit dem Adriatischen Meere beträgt ungefähr 194 m. vom Zero

Blick auf diese *Aronensia Castra*, welche gleich ein majestätisches Amphitheater darsteht, und lächelnd ein Lebewohl zuruft, und zu sagen scheint — auf baldiges Wiedersehen. Schnell geht man Lesa, Angera, Meina vo-

der erwähnten Wasserwage, die grösste Tiefe (zwischen Intra und Luino) ist 834 m. — Die des Sees von Como ist 604 m. — Die astronomische Lage des Lago Maggiore ist zwischen 26.⁰ 9.′ und 26.⁰ 31.′ Länge Ost südlich der Isola del Ferro, oder 6.⁰ 9.′ und 6.⁰ 31. Ost südlich von Paris; und zwischen 45.⁰ 45.′ und 46.⁰ 10.′ Breite nördlich. — Jahre 1868 3.ten Oktober die Wasser des Sees stiegen 7,60 m. über die Wasserwage von Pallanza, folglich die Länder am Ufer des Sees wurden überschwemmt und hatten grossen Verlust zu erleiden, glücklicher Weise war es von kurzer Dauer. — Die Wasser des Verbanos sind hell und klar, rein und himmelblau, ausgezeichnet für Bäder. — Grosse Fischerei von Packnadel *(agoni)*, Forellen, Aal und anderen Fischen. — Um den Anblik der ganzen See zu geniessen, der Reisende muss auf den Gipfel des Gallona steigen, Berg nahe bei Treffiume, Dorf welches man sieht wenn man nach *Orrido di Sant' Anna* geht. — *Sehet* **Cannobio,** *Seite* 10.

rüber und kommt in Belgirate an, woselbst
man später Gastfreiheit erhalten wird. Man
bemerkt Stresa und l' Isola Bella wohlduftende Königinn des Verbano; höher gelegen
ist Baveno und Feriolo so macht man fast
die ganze Tur der Isola Superiore und Isola
de' Pescatori (hochgelegene Insel und Fischer-
insel) bei Suna und Pallanza geht man vorüber, zärtliche Geliebte der Isolino di San
Giovanni (kleine Insel des heiligen Johanns)
welche aus den Wellen entstanden zu sein
scheinen um mit ihren Reizen die Ufern der
alten Tochter von Pallante zu verschönern.
Könnte man sich in der Mitte dieses grossen
Beckens aufhalten, hat man an einer Seite

D'un mare interminabile il cospetto

(Den grenzenlosen Anblick eines Meeres)

auf der Andern ein neues Eden. Man sieht
Intra, die kleine Manchester des Verbano und
kommt an die Festung Laveno an, welche
sich am Fusse des riesenhaftigen Sasso di
Ferro befindet ein immer interessanter Anblick

« Leva di terra al ciel nostro intelletto. »

Schnell rechts nach Porto-Valtravaglia, dann

nach Ghiffa welche sich kühn bis in die Mitte
des Sees vordrängt, als wenn sie die Hand
reichen wollte und zurufen möchte,

Come il raggio del sole ognor mi bacia,
Sì leggiadra e gentil quale mi vedi
Non m'obliare, o passeggier cortese,
Un saluto ed un bacio a me tu porta. —

(Wie der erste Sonnenstrahl mich küsst, so schön
und lieblich wie du mich siehst, vergiess mich
nicht gefälliger Reisender und ein andermal
bring mir Gruss und Kuss zu.)

Endlich ist da Oggebbio, welche reich an
schönen neuen Lustschlösser und Landhäuser
ist, unter lezteren zeichnet sich besonders la
Solitudine des Professors G. Polli aus, ungefähr zwanzig minuten höher liegt die laue
Nizza des Verbano Cannero, gesund auch in
der winterlichen Jahreszeit *. Am Oriente ist

* Wenn der Reisende Cannèro besucht, muss
er nicht unterlassen sich die Geschichte der berühmten Räuber Mazzardi oder Mazzarditi erzäh-
len zu lassen und ihr Schloss zu besuchen —
La Malpaga.

die berühmte und thätige Luino, Vaterstadt
des Bernardino Luini, *il Raffaello* der lombardischen Schule (1460-1550). Auf dem Platze
Garibaldi ist die Bildsäule des uneigennüt-
zigen Garibaldis am Fussgestelle liest man
« dem Helden der zwei Welden die Luiner.» * —
In wenig Minuten geht man bei Maccagno Inferiore und Superiore vorüber, Zwillingslän-
der welche von den Wässern des Giona ge-
trennd sind, das Erstere mit seinen Ruinen
des ehemaligen Schlosse erinnert die Pracht
und Hochmuth der Ahnen und mit Stolz zeigts
den Nahmen von Otto der Grosse, welcher
im 962 hier verweilte. Mitternächtlich geht
man bei Cannobio vorüber wo sich eine ma-
lerische Aussicht darbietet und l'Orrido di
Sant' Anna noch die berühmte Wasseranstallt
la Salute (die Gesundheit) errichtet vom
Doktor Graf Fossati-Barbò (1867-69) und
die bramentischen Zeignungen noch die Fres-
komalerei des bekannten Ferrari. Ohne es zu

* Diese Bildsäule ist vom berühmten Bildhauer
Putinati und wurde im Iahre 1867 errichtet. Sie
repräsentirt den befürchteten General im Augen-
blicke er stolz seinen Säbel schwingt; ist hoch
3 m. auf ein Fussgestell von ungefähr 4 m.

bemerken übergeht man auf dem spiegelglatten
Wasser die politische Rechtsgrenze von Italien und der Schweiz der beiden gegenüber
gelegen Punkten, Val-Mara westlich, Pino
und Cavajano östlich, hier kann man Brissago (Riva Ticinese) mit seinen sehenswerden
Sonderbarkeiten bewundern, dann lässt man
hinder sich die kleinen Inseln San Pancrazio
oder *de' Conigli* (Kaninchen) gegenüber gelegen von Ronco bemerkt man die longobar-
tische Ascona wo

Cotanto allieta del Creäto il riso

(So sehr die lächende Schöpfung erfreunt)

in der Bläue des Himmels verliehrt sich Gacta.
— Beim herumfahren des grossen Vorgebirge
von Ascona erscheint nach der Mündung, wo
sich der rauschende Maggia in den kristal-
lenen Wassern der See verliehrt, die schöne
und angenehme schweizer-italienische Haupt-
stadt des Kanton Ticino Locarno mit zwei
andern Hauptördern Lugano und Bellinzona.
Diese alterthümliche *gibelline* Locarno (welche etymologisch Wasserstadt bedeutet) zählt
12,000 Einwohner, sie ist sehenswehrt und

der Geburtsort mehreren berühmten Perso-
nen, das Schiff fährt vorüber und kommt
an den letzen Anhaltspunkt Magadino an.
Dieses ist ein sehr ungesundenes und von der
Natur wenig begünstiges Dorf, hat aber den
Vortheil der Marktplatz von der Schweiz und
Italien zu sein. Nach einer Durchfahrt von
ziemlich sechs Stunden während der man so
verschiedene Naturschönheiten bewundert hat
und die weitläufige Mündung des Ticino in
den Verbano, welcher leztere dadurch seinen
Ursprung erhielt verlassen hat, steigt man in
Belgirate ab Ziel der Reise.

Belgirate! Malerisch gelegenes Land,
betrachtet man dasselbe von der Mitte des
Sees oder von den gegenüber gelegenen Ufern
auf deren hohen und steilen Felsen das freund-
liche Ispra ruht, von der Höhe des Sasso
Ballàro, von der Einsiedelei Santa Katherine
oder von noch weiter gelegenen Punkten,
erscheint es immer von blühenden Auen und
prächtigen Gärten umgeben, ein immer blauer
reiner Himmel färbt mit seinem goldenen Lichte
dieses liebliche Land. Oh! Belgirate

È il variopinto mazzolin di fiori
Che l'onde e l'aura qui profuma ognor!

(Es ist ein Blumenstrauss welcher mit seinem Dufte Wellen und Luft erfüllt.)

Um den Anblick dieses reizenden Vorgebirge noch zu verschönern, dessen Taufsnahme Girate bene (gut auf und ab gehen) bedeutet ist es in kurzer Entfernug von Lesa und Stresa errichtet, in einem Spaziergange auf der breiten und bequemlichen Strasse des Sempione, welche auf einer Seite die See und auf der Andern dausend schöne Gärten und lächelnde 'Lustschlösser hat, ist man in zehn Minuten in der Ersteren und in drei viertel Stunde in der Anderen. Wegen der Lieblichkeit des Klimas, der gesunden Atmosphäre den ganz eigenen Reitz der Anhöhen, Hügeln und Gebirge, welche es gleich einen anmuthigen Kranz umgeben ist es sehr bekannt und wird von den berühmtesten Aerzten empfohlen als eines der ersten Oerdern, wo die Fremden jährlich Vergnügen und Gesundheit finden *. Vom Seehafen aus bemerkt man ein

* Es ist bekannt dass viele Kranke nicht vergessen können in diesem reizende Lande ihre Gesundheit gefunden zu haben noch die Gefälligkeit der Einwohner und die Dienstfertigkeit des

grossartiges Schloss an dessen Gipfel man
Hôtel Borromeo liesst *. Beim Ankommen ist

Herrn Iohann Canessa. Dieses bezeugt das Wie-
derkommen und die Dankbriefe der Fremden. —
Sehet folgende Note.

* Vor dem Iahre 1870 war es ein bescheidenes
Wirthshaus und Schafstall mit Wetterdach und
Remesse, welches den ehemaligen Grafen Borromeo als Poststation beim besuchen ihrer Inseln
am Verbano und andern Gütern diente, bis dass
der Transport auf der Strasse Monte Leone oder
Sempione durch die Eisenbahn geschehen konnte.
Heute das schöne Schloss in ein Hôtel verwan-
delt, könnte *tout bonnement* **Albergo Canessa** oder **Belgirate** genannt werden und
nicht **Hôtel Borromeo** damit die Fremden
dasselbe nicht mit dem Hôtel *Isole Borromee* in
Stresa verwechseln, was leider zu ihrem Nach-
theil oft vorkommt. Wie schon erwähnt hat es
grosse Salons im untersten Stockwerke und wenigstens 95 andere Zimmern und Kabinetten in
zwei Stockwerken nach der See sowie nach dem
Garten und Hügelgen gelegen. Salone und Zimmer
sind auf's prächtigste eingerichtet und mangelt
nichts zur Bequemlichkeit des Fremden. Hier ist
für Jedermann gesorgt, vortrefliches Billard und
andere Vergnügungen; Lesezimmer mit ausge-

man vom Hauswirth Herr Johann Canessa
freundlich empfangen, welcher schnelle und
gute Bedienung anbietet. Nachdem der durch
die reine Luft stark gewordener Apetit be-
friedigt ist und man sich in seinem, wenn auch
nicht nach der See aber nach den Garten gelegenen Zimmer bequemlich gemacht hat, oft
giebt es viel Besucher und die Zimmer nach
der See sind schon gemiethet, ist jedoch er-
zeichneten Werken in verschiedenen Sprachen.
Pianoforte und Musik fählt nicht. Ein Salon ist
für den anglican Gottesdienst bestimmt, noch
giebt es Zimmer für warme und kalte Seewasser
Bäder. — Das ganze Iahr hindurch ist das *Hôtel
Borromeo* zum Empfang der Fremden offen. Zum
Fahrten auf dem See liegen fortwährend kleine
Schiffe und elegante Goudeln bereit, Schöne und
bequeme Wagen für eins, zwei oder mehrere Pfer-
de, sind für Lustpartien stets bereit, so gar für den
Uebergang des Sempione, S. Gottardo und S. Bernardino: noch Reisebegleiter für den Motterone.
Dieser Vortheile wegen und billigen Preise, was
man nicht oft findet wird es von mehreren Fa-
milien besucht, welche mit dem Eigenthümer Herr
Canessa für die Kost überein kommen, mag es
sein für Iahr, Monat oder Woche, der Preis ist
8 bis 10 fr. täglich, nach der Lage des Zimmers.

laubt das ganze Edifizio zu jeder Stunde besuchen zu können. Vom eleganten und gut ge-
bauten Schlosse aus überschaut man noch
besser das schon bewunderte Panorama. Im
ersten Stocke, beim Eintritte des mittelen
Saals ist ein grosser Balkon von wo aus
man einen grossen Theil der Strasse des Sempione und des spiegelglatten Verbans bemerkt,
rechts, sieht man weiter als bis Arona und
Pallanza links Intra und Ghiffa. Von diesem
Balkon aus

Gira più basso il guardo,

(Wendet nieder euren Blick)

bemerkt man bequemliche und anziehende
Gegenstände welche der kluge Canessa für
Besucher zu verschönern gewusst hat. Der
kleine liebliche Garten ist reich mit wohldu-
flenden Blumen versehen, lauschige Plätzchen
und Gebüschgruppen beschützen in jeder Ta-
geszeit vor den heissen Sonnenstrahlen. Hier
bildet die reiche Natur im Verein mit be-
scheidenen Anlagen von Menschenhand ein
unvergleichliches Ganzes, so dass man ver-
sucht ist das kleine Flekchen Erde einen

Lieblingsplatz unseres Herrgottes zu nennen.
Auf dem festen eisernen Gitter sind grosse
Fakeln, welche in den warmen Sommernäch-
ten den Fremden als Leuchthurm dienen,
bei ihren Fahrten auf dem welligen Verbano.
Zum Strande hinunter führt eine grosse breite
Marmortreppe, wo zu Fahrten auf dem See
liegen fort während kleine Schiffe und Gon-
deln bereit und längs dem Ufer sind einige gute
Seebäder, zum baden sowohl als Schimmen
angelegt. Von hier aus betrachtet man das
Hôtel von seiner Morgenseite, jedes Stock hat
dreissig Fenster und die zwei Endseiten sind
etwas gebogen als ob dieses grosse Gebäute
einen Halbzirkel beschreiben möchte es ist
so sehr von Besuchern überhäuft dass mitternächtlich noch angebaut wird. Das In-
nere des Schlosses wie Saale, Zimmer und
Gemächte haben sehr fein gearbeitete Tafeln
für Gäste und herrscht die grösste Ordnung
und lässt nichts zu wünschen übrig. Die Saale
des untersten Stockwerkes (sehet vorherige
Anmerkung) welche die Aussicht nach der
See haben, können vereint werden im Falle von
grossen Mittagsessen und Zusammenkünfte.
Hier ausser den reichen Mobilien, wird die

Aufmerksamkeit des Beobachters von fünf
und dreissig feine Bildern in Anspruch ge-
nommen, es sind nicht wie es leider so oft
vorkommt unnützige und nichtssagende Vor-
stellungen, sondern erinnern den berühmten
Pinzel des Guido Reni und des viel bewein-
ten Andrea Appiani, es hätte genügt dem
kleinen einfachen Lande Bosisio, Appianius
Geburtsort (1761-1817) einen grossen Ruf zu
verschaffen, wenn es nicht schon hochberühmt
durch Parini wäre, der Prinz der Dichter
(1729-1799). — Diese fünf und dreissig Kup-
ferschnitte welche getreu die napolischen Tha-
ten, von Appiani gemald vorstellen, sind von
den vortrefflichen Longhi, Benaglia, Bisi und
Rosaspina eingeschnitten. Dem Herrn Canessa
verdankt man dass er auf diese Weise seinen
Saal zu schmücken gewusst hat und uns die
Hauptthaten der neuen Geschichte von Europa
in's Gedächtniss zurück ruft, hier, erinnert
man sich Madam d'Épinay (1725-1783). Freun-
dinn und Beschützerinn von J. J. Rousseau,
welche sagte — Dans les tableaux de l'histoire, on voit combattre et tomber des géants
puis naître et se jouer des pygmées. —
Im Lesezimmer findet man nach ermüdente

Spatziergänge und weiteren Ausflügten gute
Bücher, wenn auch schon bekannt können sie
immer Nutzen und Vergnügen verschaffen,
Voltaire hat gesagt — En lisant, pour la
première fois, un bon livre, on doit éprouver
le même plaisir que si on faisait un nouvel
ami, relire un livre qu'on a lu, c'est un ancien ami qu'on revoit. —
Nun geht man aus und lässt in Ruhe wär
frühstückt oder mittagist, wer Wegführer un-
verdauliche Romanzen, Atlasse oder Reise-
beschreibungen durchblättert, ein grüner Laub-
gang führt nach dem sehwebenden Garten,
woselbst man sich auch in der grössten Hitze
aufhalten kann. Zwei Treppen führen nach
dem Garten, ein wirklicher jardin-potager,
Nicht nur Alleen und Spaziergänge, auch allerhand wohlduftende Blumen und schöne Obst-
bäume, schmücken diesen reizenden Garten
und schattige Bäume umgeben dieses roman-
tische Labyrinth. Ein enger Weg führt noch
höher und zwar nach der alten kleinen Kirche Santa Maria Vecchia, hinter welcher man
mit Erstaunen den Friedhof von Belgirate
findet. Von dieser Höhe was für eine bezau-
bernde Aussicht! Gern möchte man hier ver-

bleiben, wenn uns nicht dieser heilige Ort
an die Sterblichkeit des Menschen erinnerte.
Rechts am Fusse sieht man das liebliche Bel- ‹
girate mit seinen reihenweise erbauten Häu-
sern, Schlösser, andere Gebäute und Gärten
alles ladet zum Besuche ein. Nichts mangelt
disem Lande, Arbeitshäuser, Werkstätte, Lä-
den, Apoteken, Kaffeehäuser, Schulen, Kinder
Freistätte welche der mütterlich gesinnten
Errichterinn Helena Conelli verdankt werden *.
Die Hauptstrasse ist der Spaziergang und
Zusammenkunftsord von allen Bewohnern, so-
gar bis nach dem romantischen Lesa. Die Pfarrkirche welche ihre Spitze in den Fluhten
des Verbans spiegelt, wurde auch von der
wohlthuenden Conelli beschenkt und zwar von

* Links der *Chiesa Vecchia* (alte Kirche) am
Kirchhof sind zwei Denkmäler, dass eine zum
Andenken der vornehmen Familie Cavallini dass
andere der Familie Conelli. (Hel. Conelli, gestor-
ben 1863). —
Die Belgiratesen werden dem verstorbenen Io-
seph Conelli ewig dankbar sein, da er sich sehr
für die Erziehung der Kinder bemühte, und lernte
denselben den Grundsatz des Helvetius — Nichts
ist für eine gute Erziehung unmöglich.

einer kostbaren Orgel von den Brüdern Bossi.
Das erste Lustschloss nach dem Hôtel war der
herbstliche Aufenthalt der lombardischen Cornelia mit ihren Söhnen, die neuen Gracchi des
vergüngten Italiens. Hier ist es wo Iohann Cairoli sterblich vom feindlichen Eisen verletzt,
seinem geliebten Vaterlande ein ewiges Lebewohl zurufte 1869! Dieses Unglück rührte
den begeisterten Philosophen Guerrazzi* welcher ein Denkmal errichtet hat, mit folgenden
rührenden Worten:

QUANDO LA SOLITUDINE DI QUESTA CASA TI PERCUOTA LA MENTE

O BENEDETTO CAIROLI

PENSA

DATO A POCHISSIMI SUPERARE LA MORTE

LA MADRE TUA E I FRATELLI IMMORTALI

PERCHÈ IMMORTALE LA RELIGIONE DI COLORO

CHE SACRARONSI INTERI

ALLA PATRIA E ALL'UMANITÀ

E CONSÓLATI

I BELGIRATESI DECRETARONO QUESTA MEMORIA IN
ONORANZA DELLA CORNELIA E DEI FATI LOMBARDI
ANNO 1872 1.º AGOSTO

* Franz Domenicus Guerrazzi der erste ge-
schichtliche Romanschreiber in Italien, berühmte

(Wenn die Einsamkeit dieses Hauses dich er-
staunt, o Benedetto Cairoli, bedenke dass es
wenigen Individuum bestimmt ist, dem Grabe
zu ünberleben. Deine Mutter und Brüder sind
unsterblich, denn unsterblich ist die Religion
derjenigen, welche dem Vaterlande und der
Menschheit ganz ergeben sind, und tröste dich).

Die Belgiratesen errichteten dieses Denkmal zum
geehrten Andenken der Cornelia und der Fabt
Lombardi, im Iahre 1872 1.en August.

Genug von diesen traurigen Erinnerungen und
richten wir unsern Weg nach Stresa, hier bemerkt man die reizende Villa der Gräfinn
Mestiatis-Castellengo mit dem schönen Thier-
garten, noch die *elegante* der Gräfinn Bisca-
rotti und das seltsame Chalet des Ministers

Gelehrte welcher für die Freiheit kämpfte, geb:
Livorno 1805 gest: 1873. 23.ten September, in seiner *Villa Cinquantina, nel Eitto di Cécina* bei Livorno. L'*Assedio di Firenze*, vorzügliches Werk
welches allgemein bekannt ist, schrieb er im Ge-
fängniss der Festung *Stella di Portoferraio* worin
Guerrazzi geworfen wurde, strafbar sein Vater-.
land zu sehr zu lieben! (1834).

Bonghi; wenig Schritte davon ist die berühmte
Villa Donavaro gelegen. Unmöglich nicht in
dieses irdische Paradis einzutreten. — Viele
Iahre gehörte dieses prachtvolle Lustschloss,
welches *Villa dei due riali* wegen den beiden
Kleinen durchgehenden Flüssen genannt wurde, dem edlen Markis von Brême an; jetzt
ist sie Eigenthum des Herrn Danovaro von
Genua, welcher dieselbe in einen Garten der
Esperidi zu verwandeln wusste, gleich ein
neuer und süsser Aufenthalt der Göttinn Ca-
lipso. — In diesem schönen Orte bewundert
man den fruchtbaren Boden, die Pflege und
Aufmerksamkeit des Gärtners. Ausländische
oder inländische Pflanzen, Blumen, Bäumchen,
Sträucher, alles hat hier geil Wurzel gefasst,
um jede Ecke dieses lieblichen Aufenthalts zu
verschönern. Indem man so das Heiligthum der
Göttinn Flora bewundert, bemerkt man einen
Wald von hohen, stolzen Bäumen wie Tannen-
zapfen, Lorbeerbäume, der wohlduftende Kam-
pherlorbeerbaum und andere ausländische Bäume, welche sich hier ganz einheimisch finden.
Kleine Flüsse, Grotten in den einsamsten Fle-
cken, einen Fischteich mit schönen goldge-
färbten Fischchen umgeben von weissen Mar-

morbildsäulen, welche vier dichterische Gott-
heiten vorstellen Frühling, Sommer, Herbst
und Winter nebst andere viere Europa, Asien,
Afrika und Amerika. — Der übrige Platz ist
mit Turniers, Schauckeln, Karrousells und
allerhand ähnliche Vergnügungen versehen.
Auch hier der befruchtende Hauch des Zefyrs
vermählt sich mit seiner geliebten Blumen-
göttinn, Blumen und Pflanzen athmen die reine
Luft ein und scheinen eifersüchtig über das
Glück der beiden Geliebten zu sein! Welch
Wohlgeruch, welche erfreuente Wollust! —
Man muss sich in Acht nehmen während man
die unbekannten Wegen verfolgt, in eine ma-
lerische Grotte oder Tunnel eintritt und mit
Erstaunen diese Merkwürdigkeiten, sowie kleine mit Grün geschmückte Tempel Gewächs-
häuser oder künstlich errichtete Ruinen bewundert, wird man mit Wasser bespritzt, als
ob man eine unerwartete Taufe von den Wassern des Weltmeers erhielt. Nach dieser freund-
lichen Begrüssung übergeht man blühende
Wiesen welche die Luft mit Wohlduft erfüllen und mit Zärtlichkeit zu sagen scheinen. —
Tretet nicht auf diese Blumen, wenn sie Euch
so viel Vergnügen verschaffen =

Non calpestarci se ti siam cortesi.

Dieser Ort ist so mit lieblichen Blumen über-
sämmt dass man, nicht ohne Verdruss, oft
diese lebende Wesen zertritt; Bernardin de
Saint-Pierre sagte, eine Blume ist interessanter als ein Stern und der kleinste Garten
mehr als das Firmament. Beim Anblicke so
vieler von Allen geliebten Blumen, welche

Di soäve ristoro a quei che passa,

im innersten der Seele uns mit Zärtlichkeit
und Lust erfüllen, verlässt man ungern diesen
schönen Ort und vergisst nie

„ Le elette cose che il bel loco serra! „

Weiter nach Stresa giebt es noch grosse und
kleinere Lustschlössser, welche die Ufern des
Verbanos zieren, man bemerkt das schöne
noch nicht geendigte Schloss, welches der anmuthige Aufentshaltort der reichen Familie
Palestrini sein wird, die Baukunst macht dem
Ingenieur Defendente Vanini viel Ehre. Dann
die grosse immer blühende Villa Fulvia ehe-

mals der Prinzessinn Mathilde Bonaparte an-
gehörend; noch die schöne Vignolo des En-
gländers Herr Nixon, einige Schritte weiter
die anmuthige Villa Pallavicino, ein anderes
schönes Paradies. Diesen Weg so fortgehend
kommt man in Stresa an, beliebter Aufenthalt der Besucher und Einwohner, viele grosse
und schöne Gebäude, am Ende des Dorfes die
grossartige Villa der Könniglichen Hoheit Her-
zoginn von Genua Mutter der vielgeliebten *Prinzessinn Margarethe* welche später als Edel-
stein in der Krone von Italien glänzen wird. —
Beim Zurückgehen werden neue Schönheiten
bemerkt, man begreift aber dass unser *Blick
nach Belgirate* unendlich sein würde da sich
alle Tage noch nicht bemerkte Sehenswer-
thigkeiten darbieten, man wird seiner Mühe
reichlich belohnt denn *voyager*, *c'est apprendre*. —

Alle Reisende behaupten Belgirate ein Zu-
sammenkunftsort, wo die Natur und Kunst
sich die Hand geben. Harmonisches Ganze,
welches edle Seelen mit Wonne erfüllt, ge-
fühlvolle Seelen lieben das Schöne mit dem
Nützlichen verbunden, hier bleibt man. Um
einen wirklich prachtvollen Anblick zu ge-

niessen muss man den Sonnenaufgang auf den
hohen Bergen erwarten, hier die mit ewigen
Schnee bedeckten Spitzen der Alpen, dort eine
unbeschränkte Weite wo sich der Horizont im
Unendlichen verliehrt dessen blauer und reiner Himmel Lust macht gleich ein Vogel
durch die Luft fliegen zu können, um diese
üppige Schöpfung besser zu beobachten. —
Am Tage sowie Nachts muss man ausgehen,
um die schnell übergangenen Länder |besser
zu betrachten, wenn auch Belgirate uns nicht
geschichtberühmte Ahnen aufweisen kann, we-
der nichtssagende und oft falsche Reliquien,
noch alterthümliche Schlösser, traurige Ueber-
bleibe wo einst die Bosheit der Herzogen und
Baronen herrschte, sondern mit edlen Stolz
zeigt es uns seine Thätigkeit, Kunstfleiss, Com-
merzio, die Fruchtbarkeit seiner gesegnenten
Erde, wo die Belgiratesen süsse Früchte und
ausgezeichneten Wein zu pflegen wissen.

Belgirate von Pallanza umgeben gehört
dem Mandat von Lesa zu, kleiner aber interessanter Hauptort, welcher sich in wenigen
Iahren Ruf zu verschaffen gewusst hat. Die
Belgirateser eifersüchtig von der Thätigkeit
und Verschönerung der benachbarden Ländern,

bemühten sich diese nach zu ahmen und woll-
ten auch auf ihrem Wappen die drei **O** von
Teodoro de Bèze als Symbolum derselben
Treue — **Opus, Opes, Ops** — dass heisst
Arbeit, Reichthum, Sorgfallt, welches Franklin so erklärte. — Verarmt wer zu lange
schläft; verschafft sich Gesundheit, Reichthum
und Kenntnisse wer früh aufsteht. —

O italienische Provinzen, amth diese Sees
Bewohner nach!

ENDE

www.ingramcontent.com/pod-product-compliance
Lightning Source LLC
Chambersburg PA
CBHW031246260626
47169CB00007B/2464